For my mom.—A. C. R.

For those with dreams of grand adventures.—I. S.

Text copyright © 2019 Annie Cronin Romano
Illustrations copyright © 2019 Ileana Soon

First published in 2019 by Page Street Kids,
an imprint of
Page Street Publishing Co.
27 Congress Street, Suite 105
Salem, MA 01970
www.pagestreetpublishing.com

Distributed by Macmillan, sales in Canada by The Canadian Manda Group

19 20 21 22 23 CCO 5 4 3 2 1

ISBN-13: 978-1-62414-657-2
ISBN-10: 1-624-14657-0

CIP data for this book is available from the Library of Congress.

This book was typeset in Acre.
The illustrations were done digitally.

Printed and bound in China

Page Street Publishing uses only materials from suppliers who are committed to
responsible and sustainable forest management.

Page Street Publishing protects our planet by donating to nonprofits like The Trustees,
which focuses on local land conservation.

Night Train

A JOURNEY FROM DUSK TO DAWN

Annie Cronin Romano · illustrated by Ileana Soon

PAGE STREET KIDS

Night train

wakens

to the dusk,

groggy,

stretching,

load and roll,

     load and roll.

Locomotive roars to life.

Journey starting,

day departing—

pulling, straining, coal-containing night train.

Night train labors through the hills,

surely winding,

back and forth,

back and forth.

Pine trees wave their spiny branches.

Wheels a-clatter, creatures scatter—

hissing, chugging, mountain-hugging night train.

Night train rolls along the plains,

ever moving,

straight and speedy,

straight and speedy.

Wheat fields sway their golden greetings.

Boxcars rattle, spooking cattle—

steady crawling, never-stalling night train.

Night train rumbles by the creek,

brakeman watching,

chug and huff,

chug and huff.

Icy currents splash in rhythm.

Chimney billows, bending willows—

water-racing, river-chasing night train.

Night train chugs by whitewashed barns,

hot coal burning,

puff and steam,

  puff and steam.

Iron horse against the stallions.

Full moon glitters, brown bat flitters—

rivals trailing, rarely failing night train.

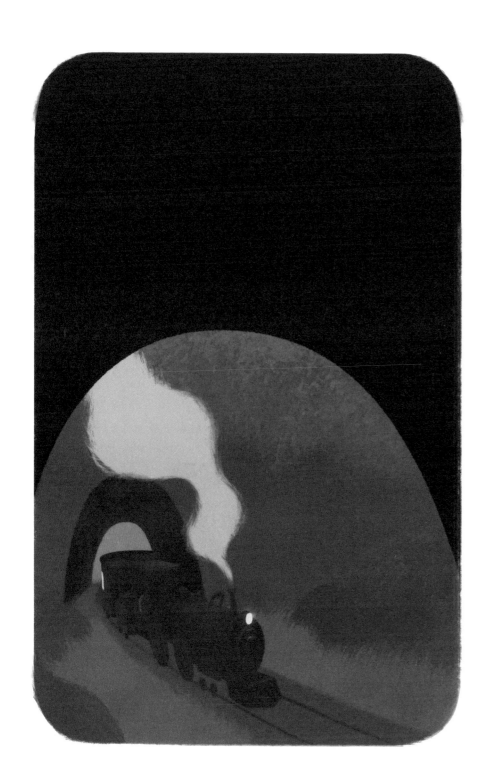

Night train steams through tunnels black,

never swaying,

in and out,

    in and out.

Granite passage hides the railway.

Headlamp brightens, pathway lightens—

never-fearing, calmly steering night train.

Night train wakes the drowsy town,

pistons grinding,

squeal and creak,

squeal and creak.

Sleepy children count the boxcars.

Workmen hurry, stray cats scurry—

folks awaking, engine-quaking night train.

Night train shakes the station walls,

brakes a-screeching,

slow and stop,

   slow and stop.

Worn conductor yawns and stretches.

Journey finished,

dark diminished—

sunlight streaming,

finally

dreaming

night train.